A special thanks to my
little sister Natasha,
and Mom and Dad

— Tatiana

BOOK DESIGN BY CRYSTAL KINNEY

Published by
Kids Publishing - "For Kids By Kids"
(713) 977-1111
Printed in China
First Printing 10 9 8 7 6 5 4 3 2

Library of Congress Catalog Data Available
Mommy, Mommy, Mommy! / Tatiana Reger
Summary: A young girl learns the importance of having her Dad.
ISBN 0-9778065-2-9

MOMMY MOMMY MOMMY!

author
Tatiana Reger

illustrator
Tatiana Reger & Crystal Kinney

KIDS PUBLISHING

Mommy in the morning

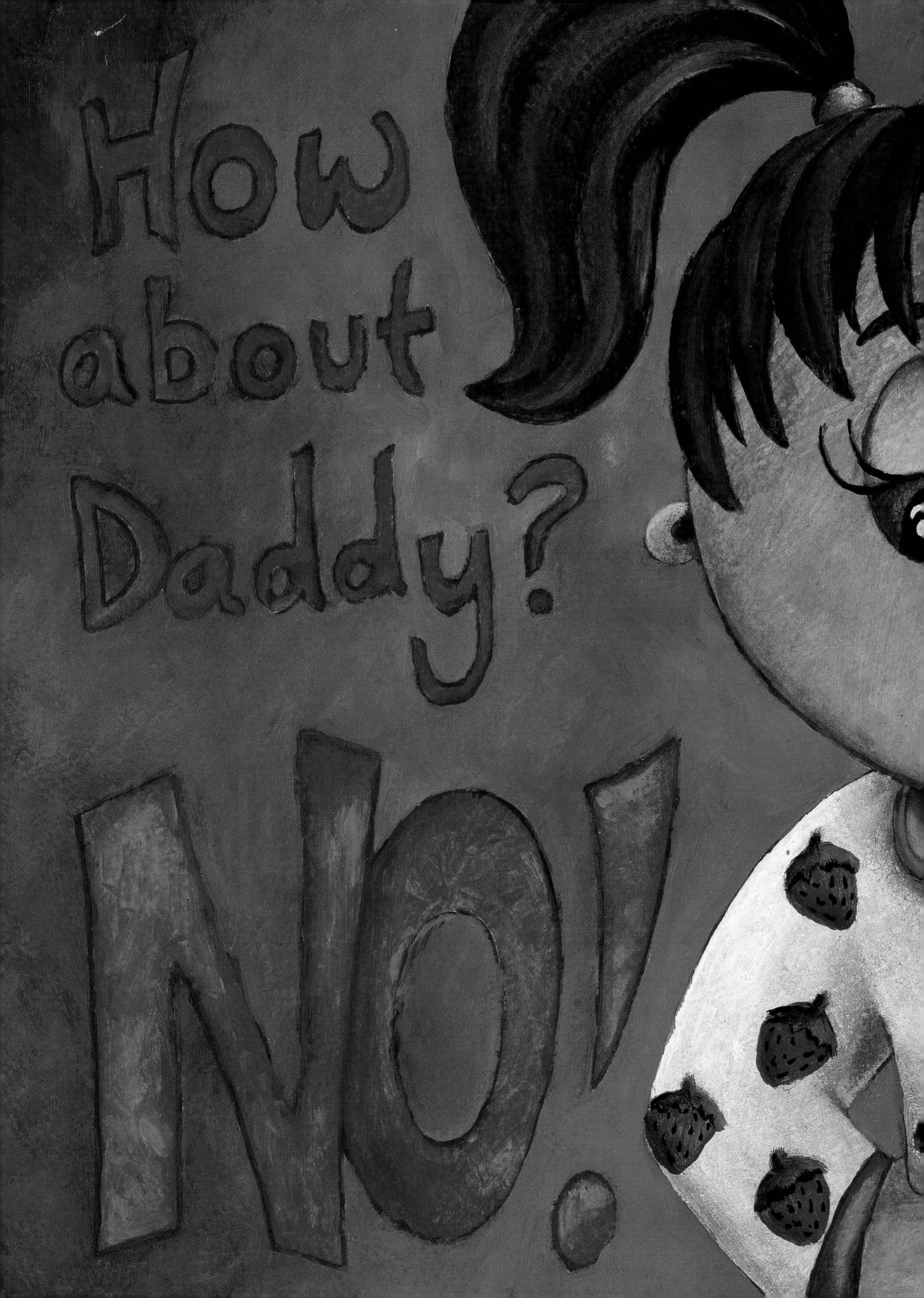
How about Daddy?
NO!

Mommy
in the
bathroom

Mommy
in the

house

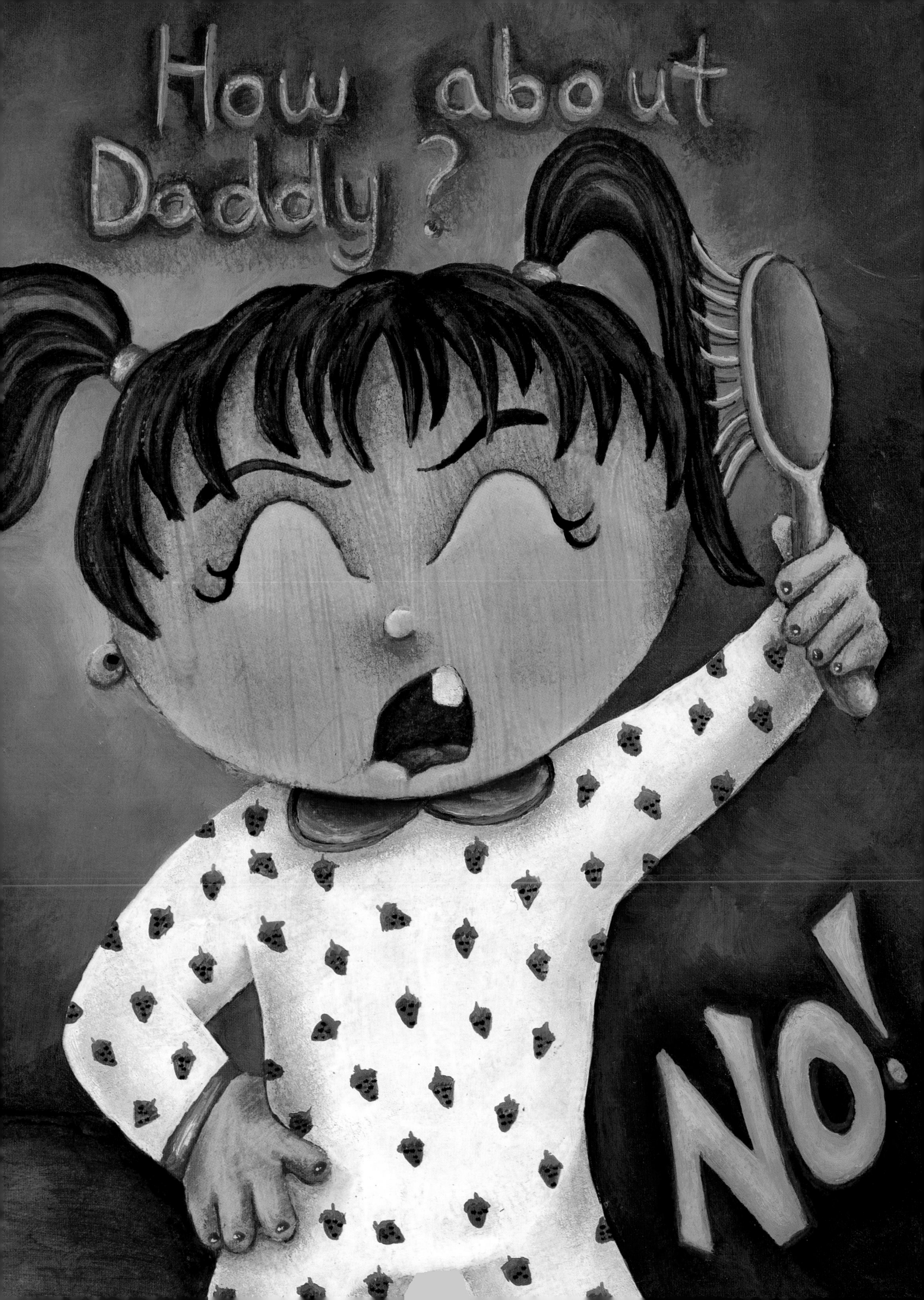
How about Daddy?
NO!

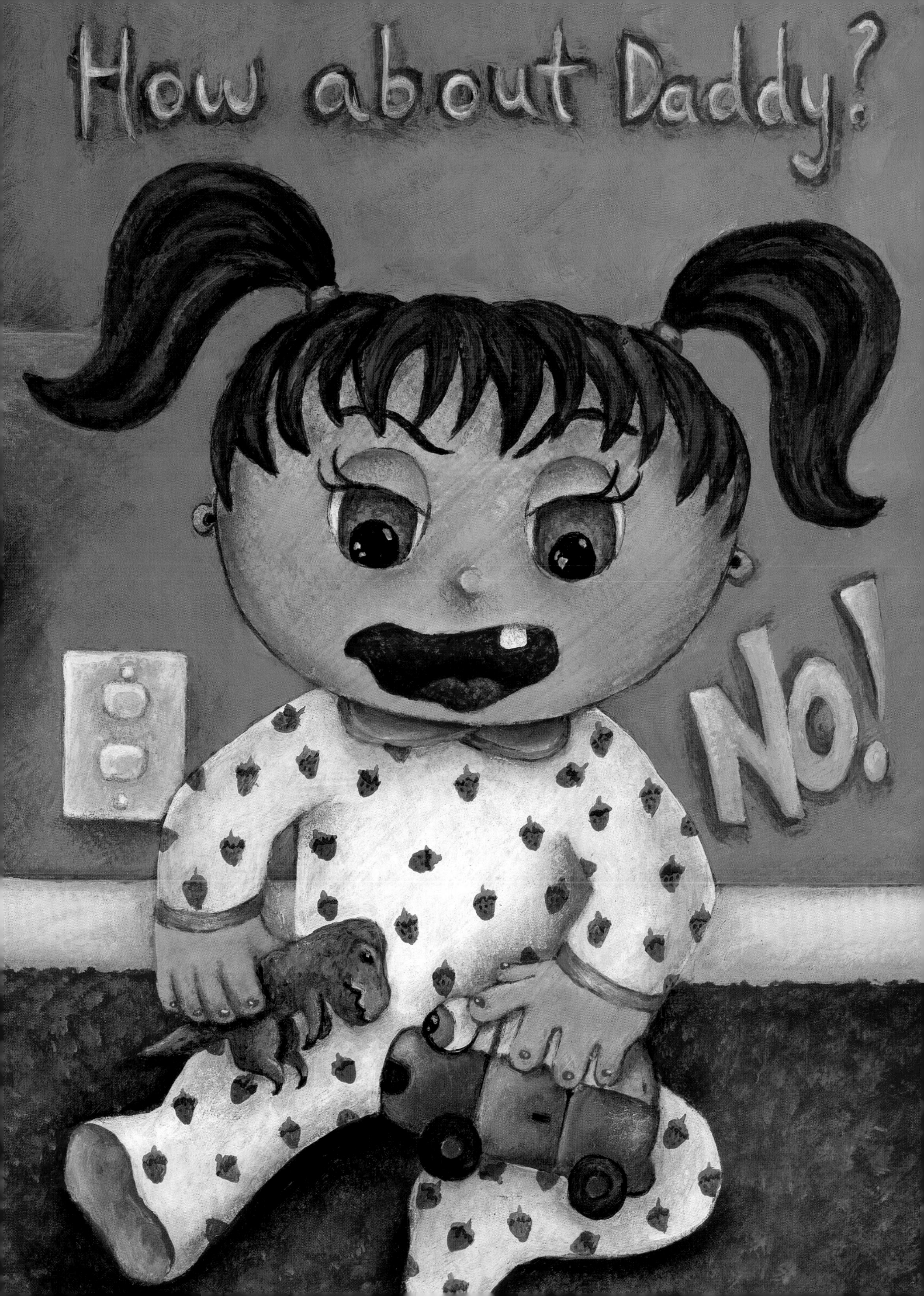
How about Daddy?
NO!

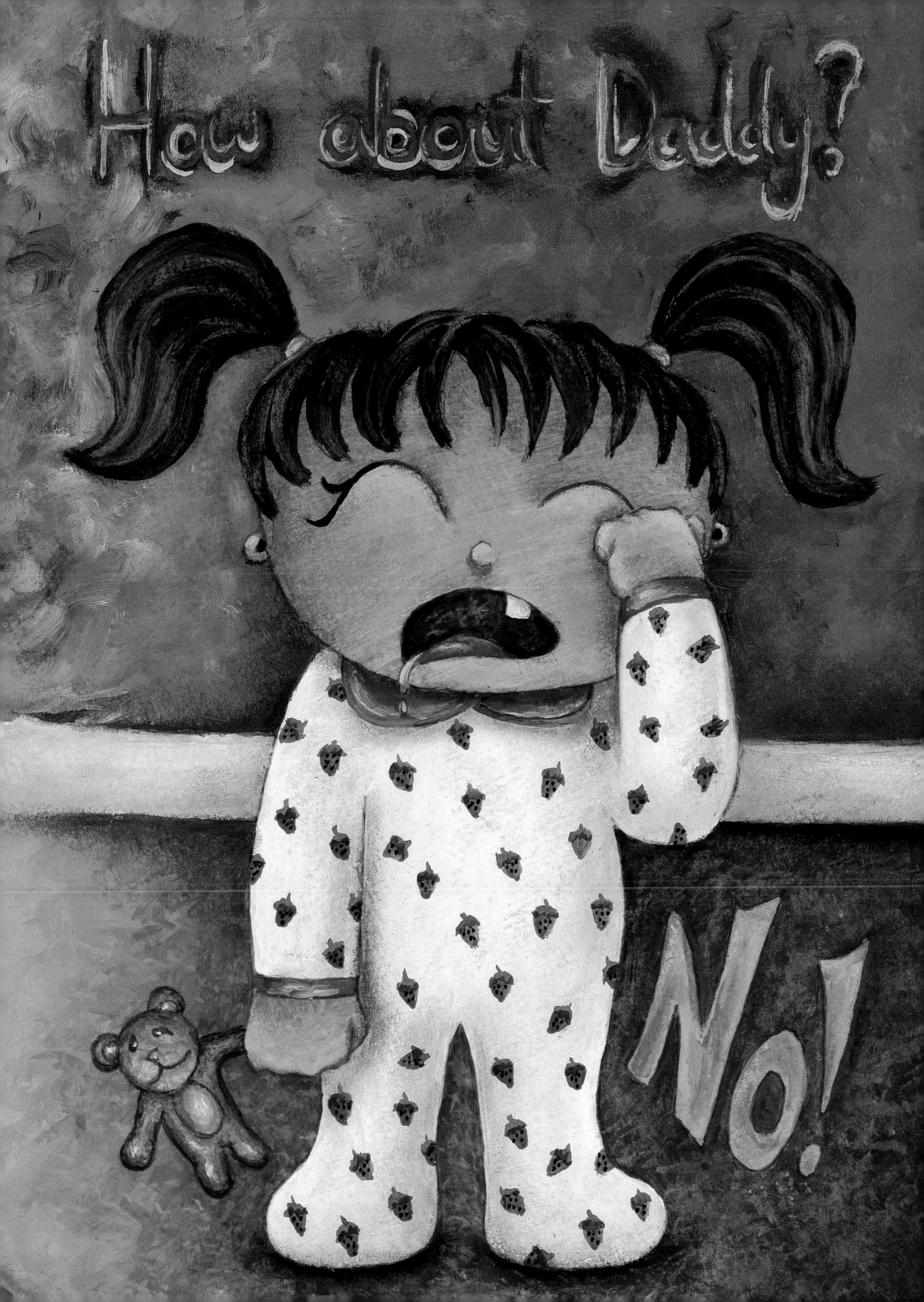
How about Daddy?
No!

Live your dreams!

A NOTE FROM THE AUTHOR

I dedicate this book to my baby sister, Natasha. She is the best thing that happened in my life, especially after having three younger brothers first. I thought my dream of having a sister would never come. I wanted to portray her cuteness when she was only 18 months old. My illustrations will tell it all: her pig-tails and attitude towards my dad. Even though she yells out "Mommy, Mommy, Mommy!" she is still daddy's little girl after all. I hope that you have enjoyed this book as much as I had writing it, and that it will be an inspiration for you and others around the world who would like to live out their dreams of becoming an author. If you have a great story you would like to have published, contact the company that specializes in young authors.

I look forward to seeing your book soon!

- Tatiana Reger

For more about getting published, go to
KIDSPUBLISHING.ORG
(713) 977-1111

KIDSPUBLISHING.ORG

OTHER BOOKS BY THE AUTHOR

• MOMMY, MOMMY, MOMMY!

• JUST ONE PENNY

• MY TEACHER'S

TATIANA REGER & VUTHY KUON

JUST ONE PENNY

Hi! My name is Tatiana and I'm 9 years old!

The End